# SUPERGIRL: Girl of Steel

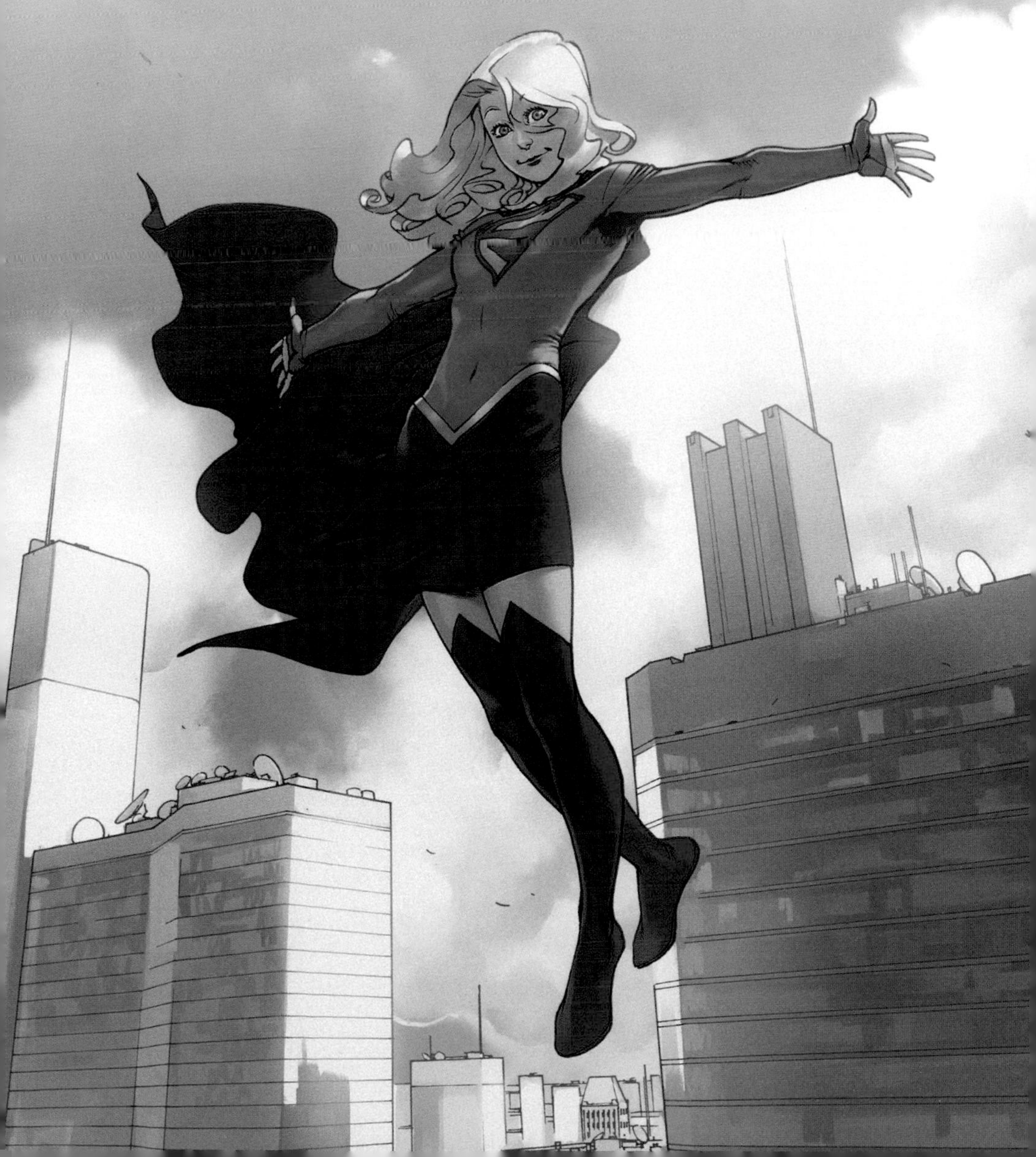

**Editor** Frankie Hallam
**Project Art Editor** Jon Hall
**Designer** Thelma-Jane Robb
**Proofreader** Julia March
**Senior Production Editor** Siu Yin Chan
**Senior Production Controller** Mary Slater
**Managing Editor** Emma Grange
**Managing Art Editor** Vicky Short
**Publishing Director** Mark Searle

**Reading Consultant** Barbara Marinak

First American Edition, 2023
Published in the United States by DK Publishing
1745 Broadway, 20th Floor, New York, NY 10019

Page design copyright © 2023 Dorling Kindersley Limited
DK, a Division of Penguin Random House LLC
23 24 25 26 27  10 9 8 7 6 5 4 3 2 1
001– 334315–Jun /2023

Based on the characters created by Jerry Siegel and Joe Shuster.
By special arrangement with the Jerry Siegel family.

A catalog record for this book is available from the Library of Congress.
ISBN: 978-0-7440-8171-8 (Paperback)
ISBN: 978-0-7440-8172-5 (Hardcover)

DK books are available at special discounts when purchased in bulk for sales promotions,
premiums, fund-raising, or educational use. For details, contact: DK Publishing Special Markets,
1745 Broadway, 20th Floor, New York, NY 10019
SpecialSales@dk.com

ACKNOWLEDGMENTS
DK would like to thank Ruth Amos, Cefn Ridout, and Sophie Dryburgh for their help and expertise.

Printed and bound in China

For the curious
**www.dk.com**

# SUPERGIRL: Girl of Steel

Frankie Hallam

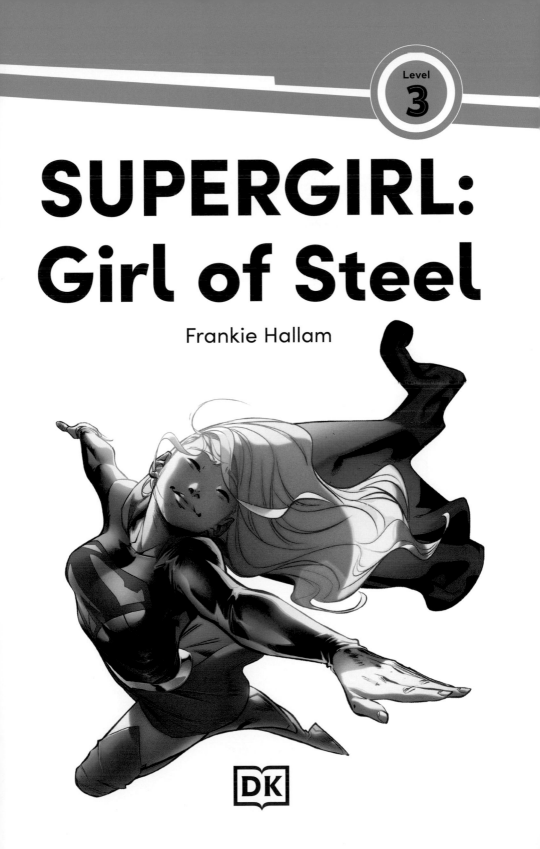

DK

# Contents

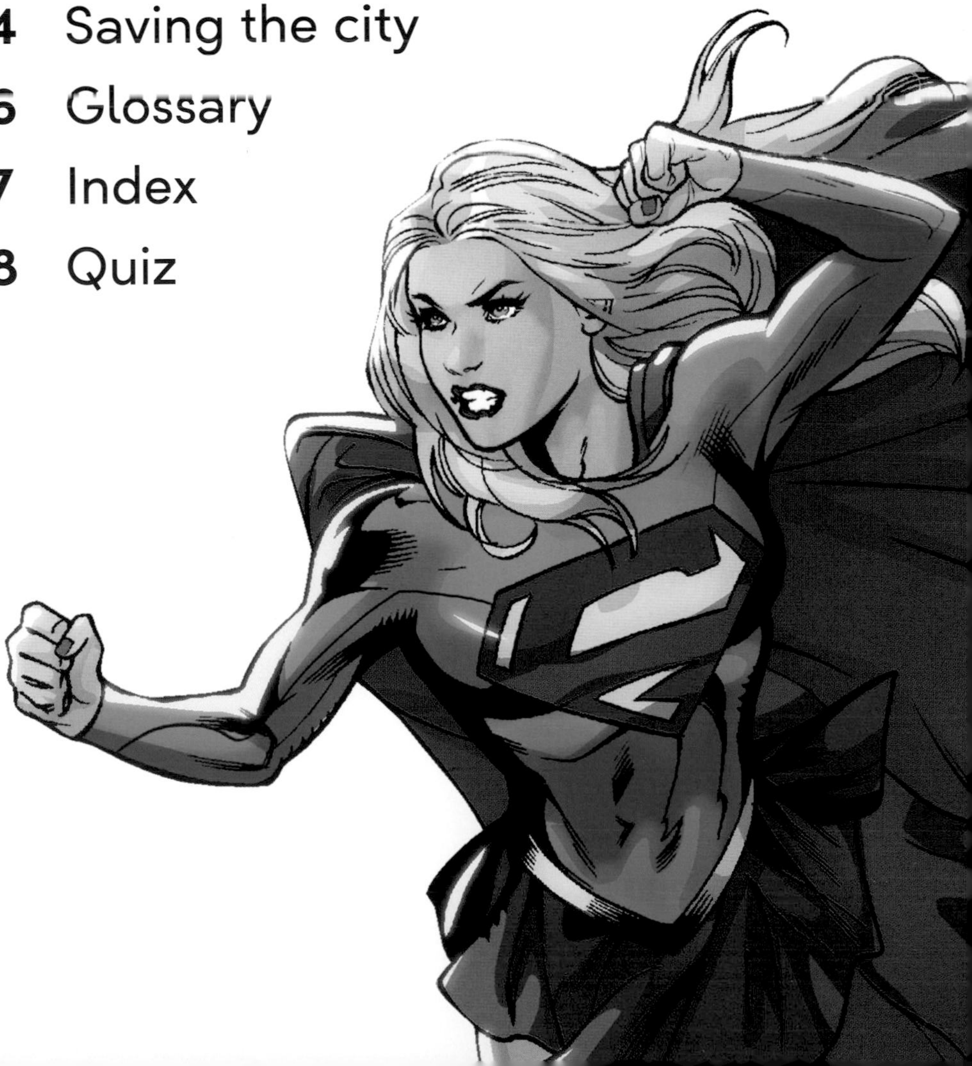

# Meet Supergirl

Supergirl is a true Super Hero. She is known as the "Girl of Steel" because she is incredibly strong. She also has other amazing powers, such as super-vision, and the ability to fly.

Above all, Supergirl is brave and fights for justice and peace across the universe.

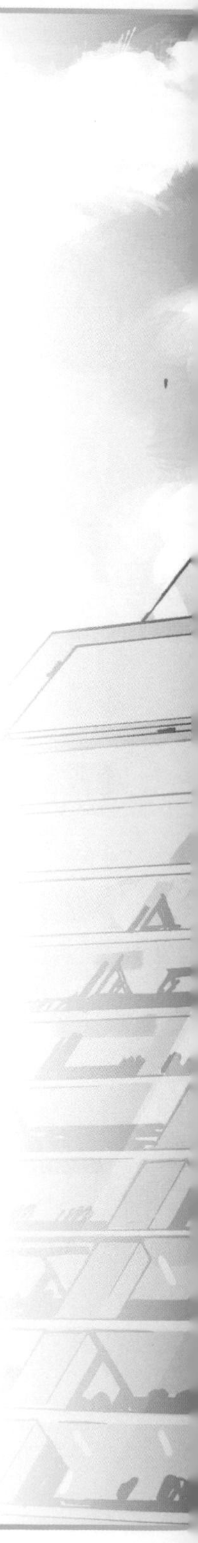

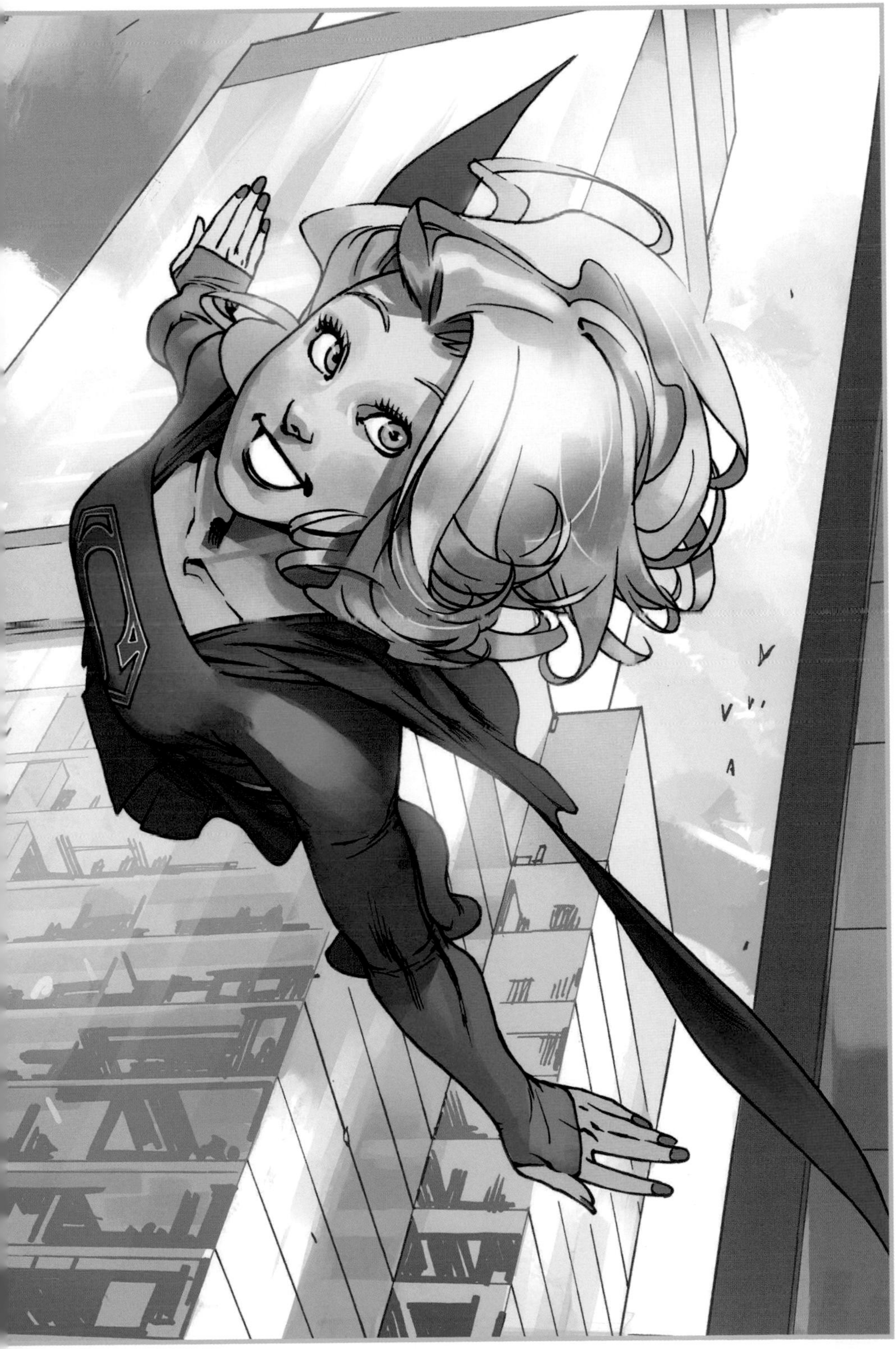

# Supergirl's origins

Supergirl's real name is Kara Zor-El. She was born on a faraway planet called Krypton. Kara was sent to Earth in a spaceship when Krypton was destroyed in an explosion.

She had to be brave when she left her mother and father behind. Kara misses Krypton, but her powers are needed more on Earth!

# Secret identity

Supergirl hides her true identity on Earth to protect those who are close to her. She uses the name Kara Danvers, turns her hair color from blonde to brown, and wears glasses. When Kara becomes Supergirl, nobody can recognize her.

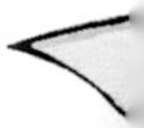

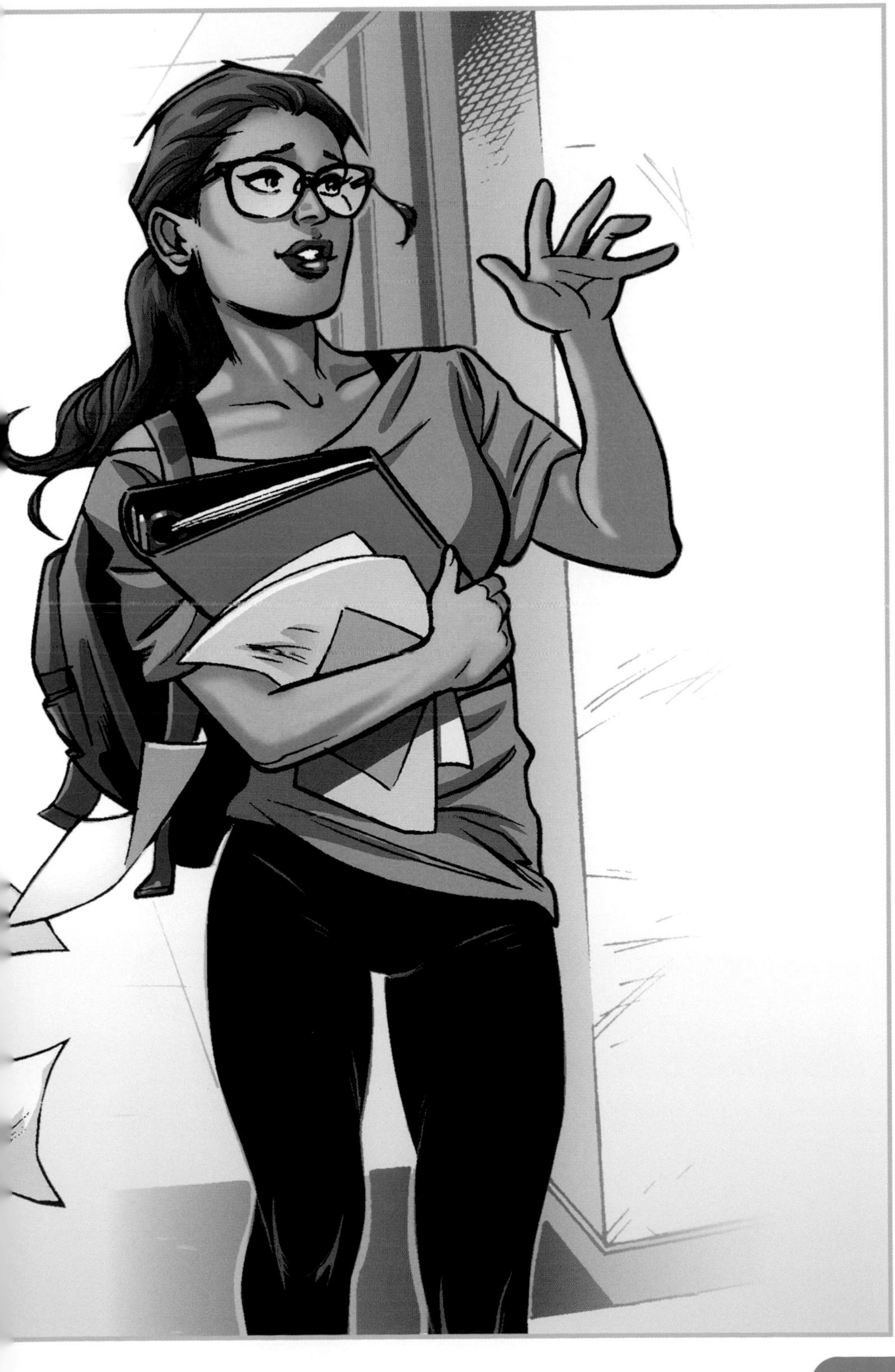

# Working Life

Kara lives in National City in California, USA, and attends National City Technical High School. This is a special school for students who are good at science.

**National City Technical High School**

**Department of Extranormal Operations (DEO)**

Supergirl also works with the Department of Extranormal Operations (DEO). The DEO protects Earth from alien threats. Supergirl is important because she is from another planet. She has knowledge that no one else does.

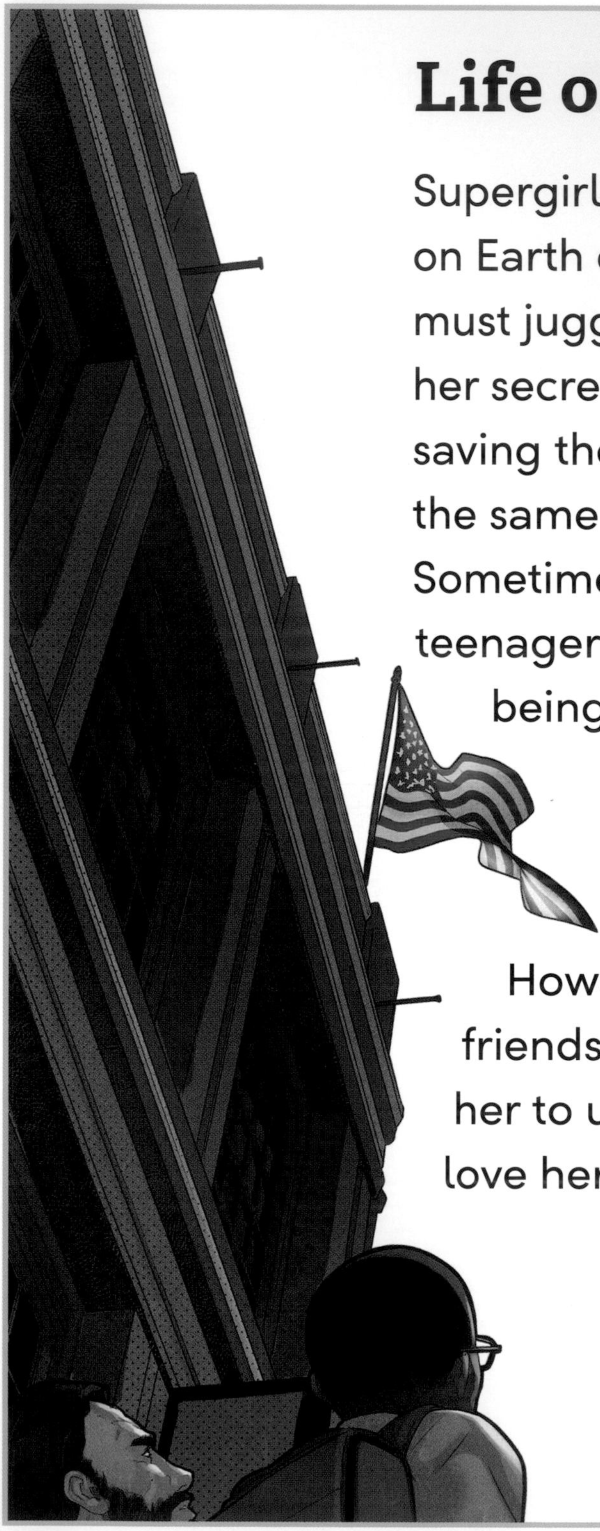

# Life on Earth

Supergirl often finds life on Earth difficult. She must juggle homework, her secret identity, and saving the world, all at the same time. Sometimes being a teenager is harder than being a Super Hero!

However, Kara's friends and family help her to understand and love her new planet.

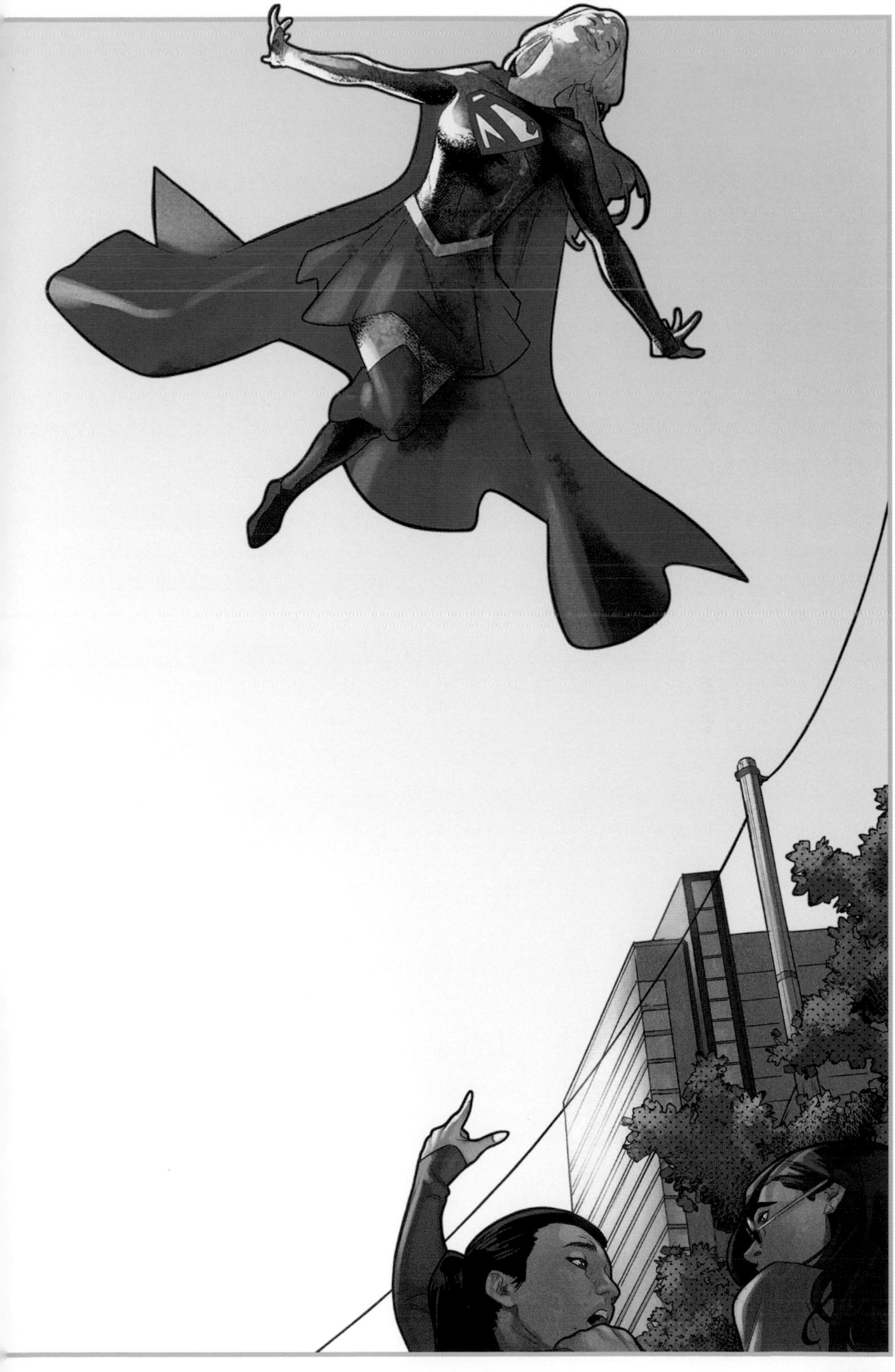

# Family on Earth

Kara's foster parents are Eliza and Jeremiah Danvers. They are also DEO agents and often help Kara on her missions. They try to make her feel happy on Earth, because Kara misses Krypton. Over time, Jeremiah and Eliza begin to feel like family to Kara.

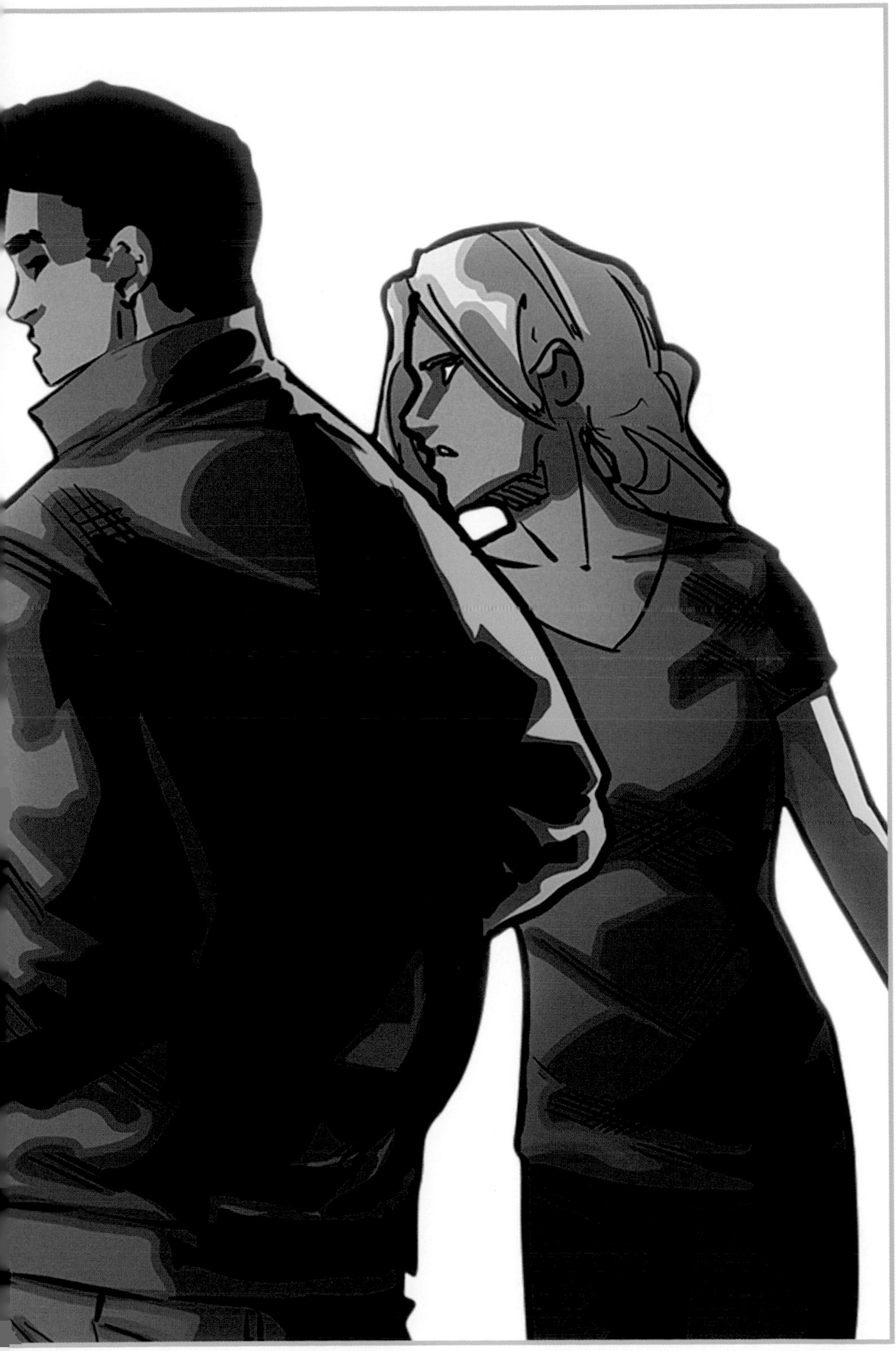

# Supergirl's superpowers

Supergirl gains many awesome powers from Earth's yellow sun. Here are some of her abilities.

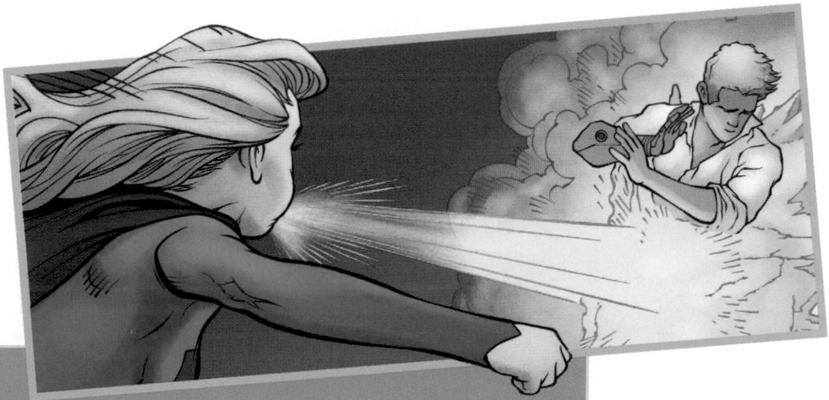

**Super-breath**
She can use her breath to freeze her enemies in one big whoosh!

**Super-hearing**
Supergirl can hear trouble from many miles away.

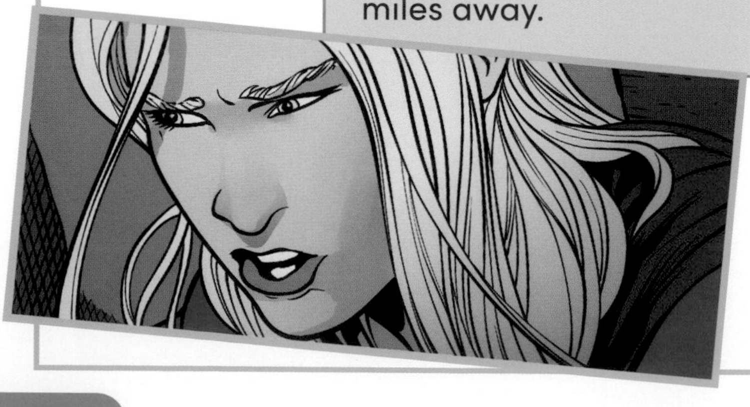

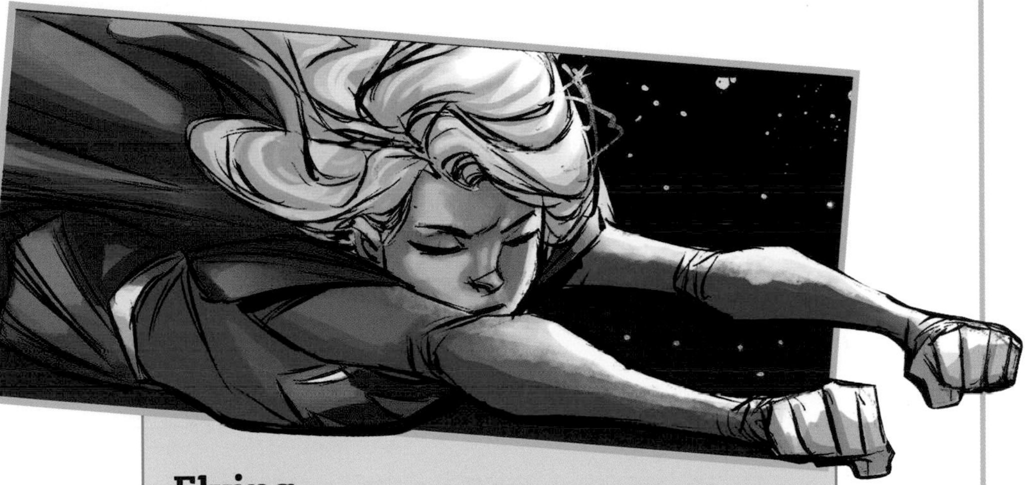

**Flying**
Supergirl doesn't need a spaceship, she can use her powers to fly among the planets and the stars.

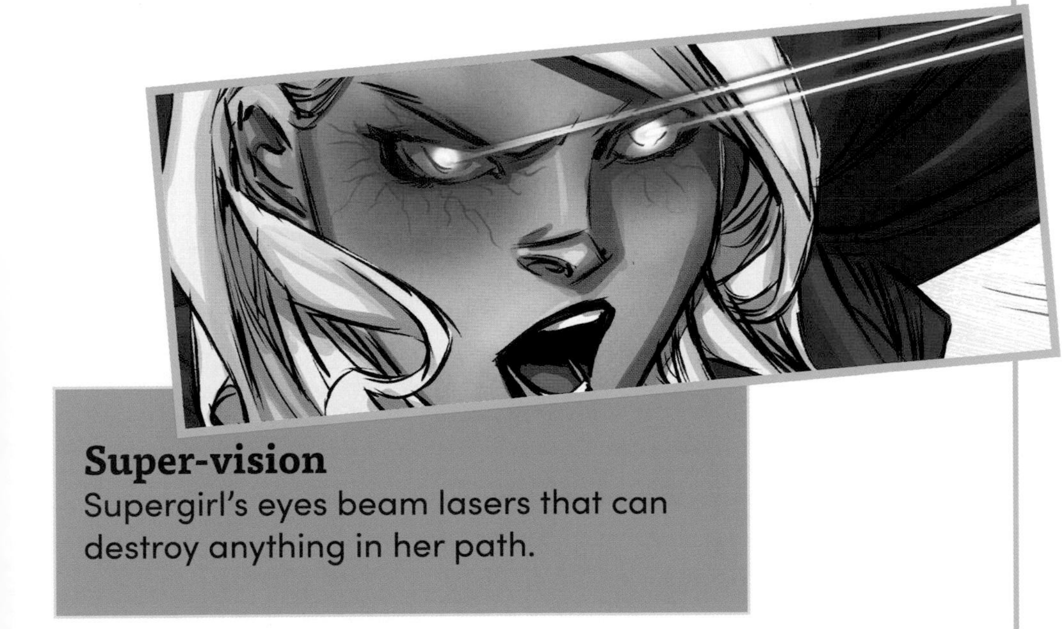

**Super-vision**
Supergirl's eyes beam lasers that can destroy anything in her path.

# Supergirl's suit

Supergirl's suit is made out of Kryptonian fabric. It can handle really hot or cold temperatures. It protects Supergirl when she needs it the most. Her cape also helps her to fly through the skies. Watch her go!

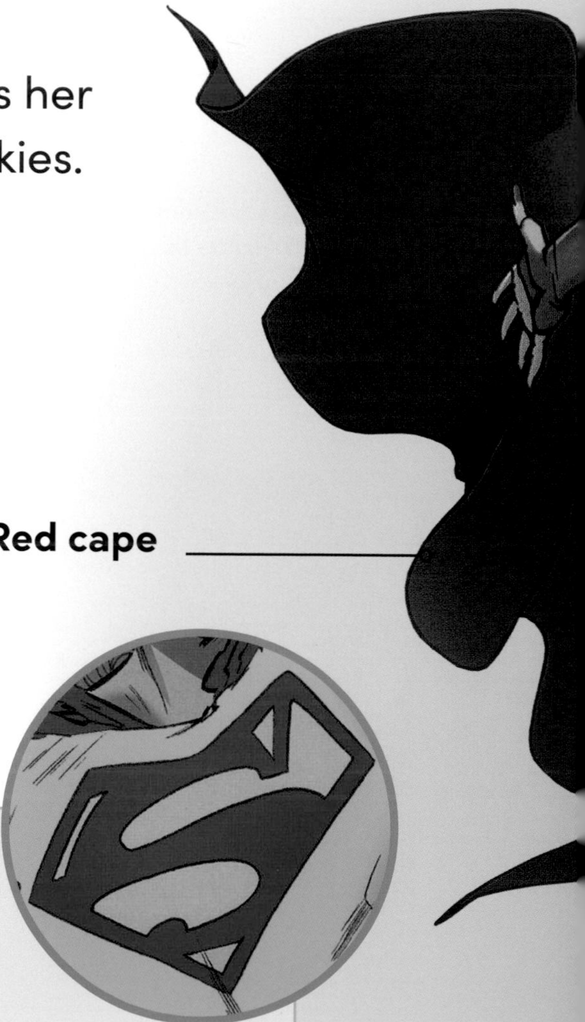

Red cape


**S-shield**
Supergirl's suit has an S-shield, just like her cousin Superman's.

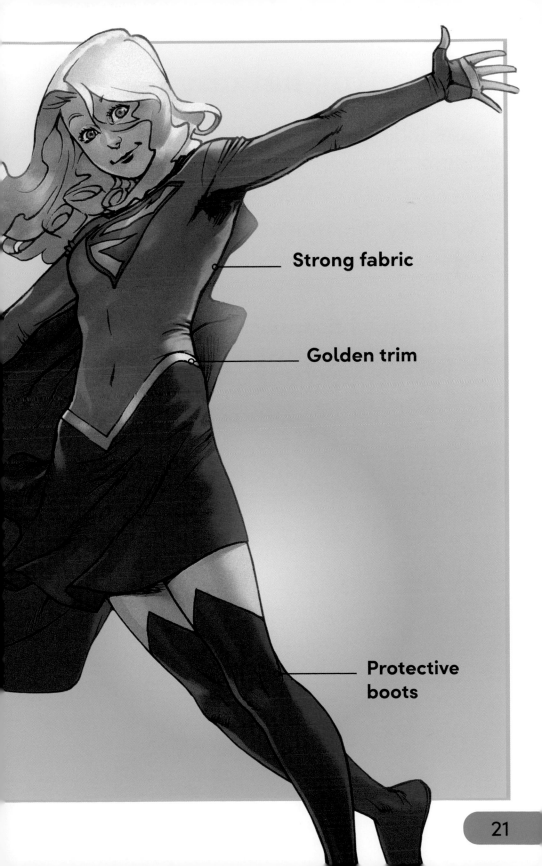

**Strong fabric**

**Golden trim**

**Protective boots**

# Protecting her city

Supergirl always protects her city from danger, whatever the cost. It has become her home, and its people are her family. Supergirl gives hope to National City.

Fighting for peace across the universe is just another day's work for Supergirl.

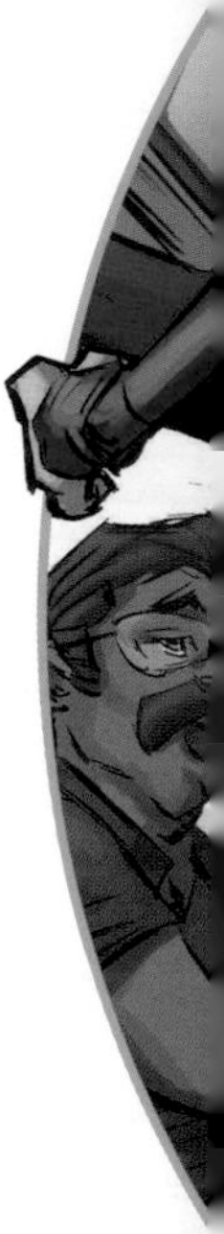

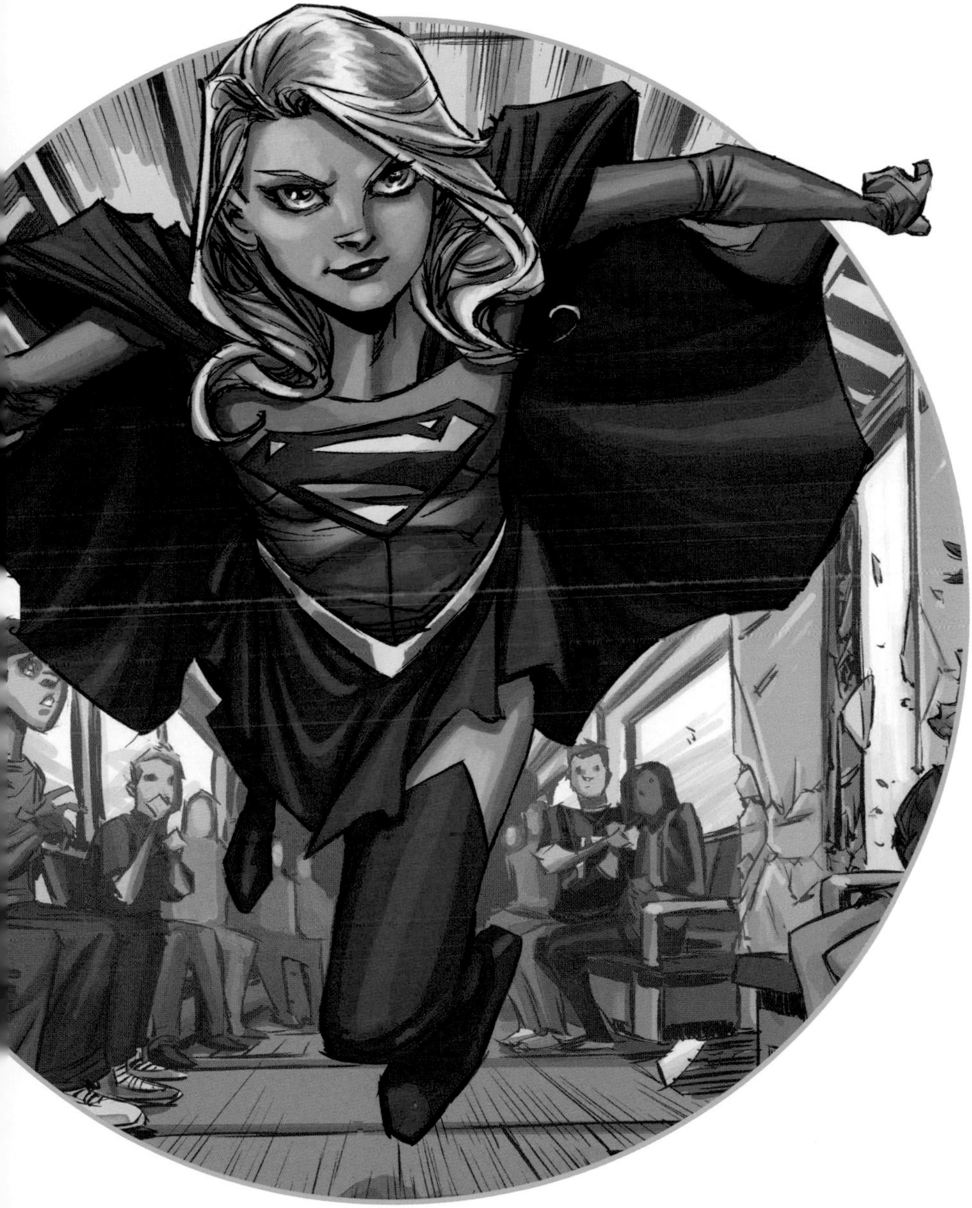

# Supergirl and Superman

Kara's cousin was also sent to live on Earth. He was only a baby when he arrived. You might have heard of him; his name is Superman. Superman has some of the same amazing powers as Supergirl. Superman and Supergirl always look out for each other. When they join forces, nothing can stop them.

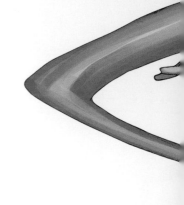

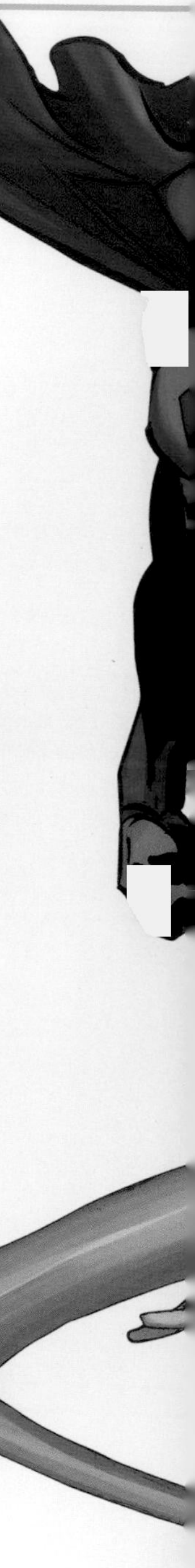

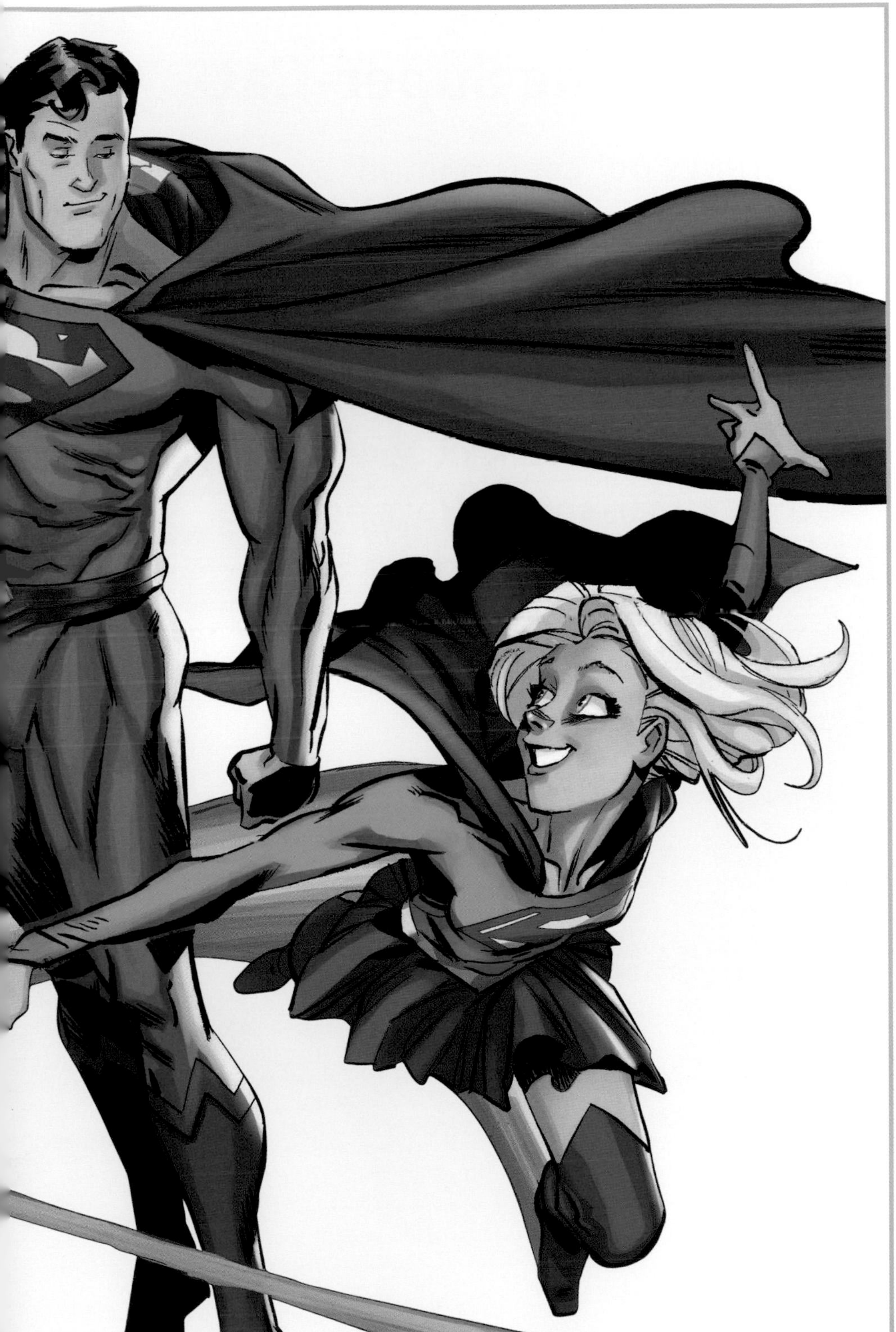

# Streaky the Super-Cat

Supergirl's pet cat is named Streaky. He has lightning bolt marks on his red fur. One day, Streaky was exposed to a type of crystal called X-Kryptonite. This gave him lots of special powers, such as super-speed. He is part of a group of animals called the Super-Pets. Streaky would do anything to keep Supergirl safe. He is fluffy and fearless!

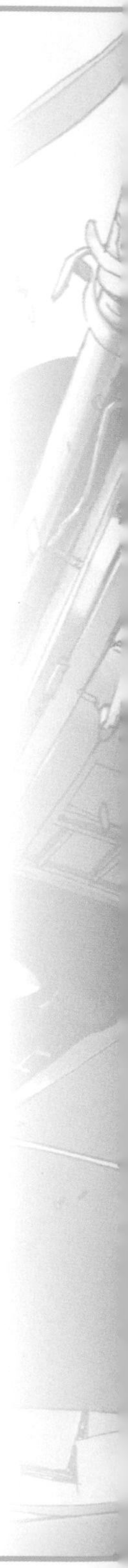

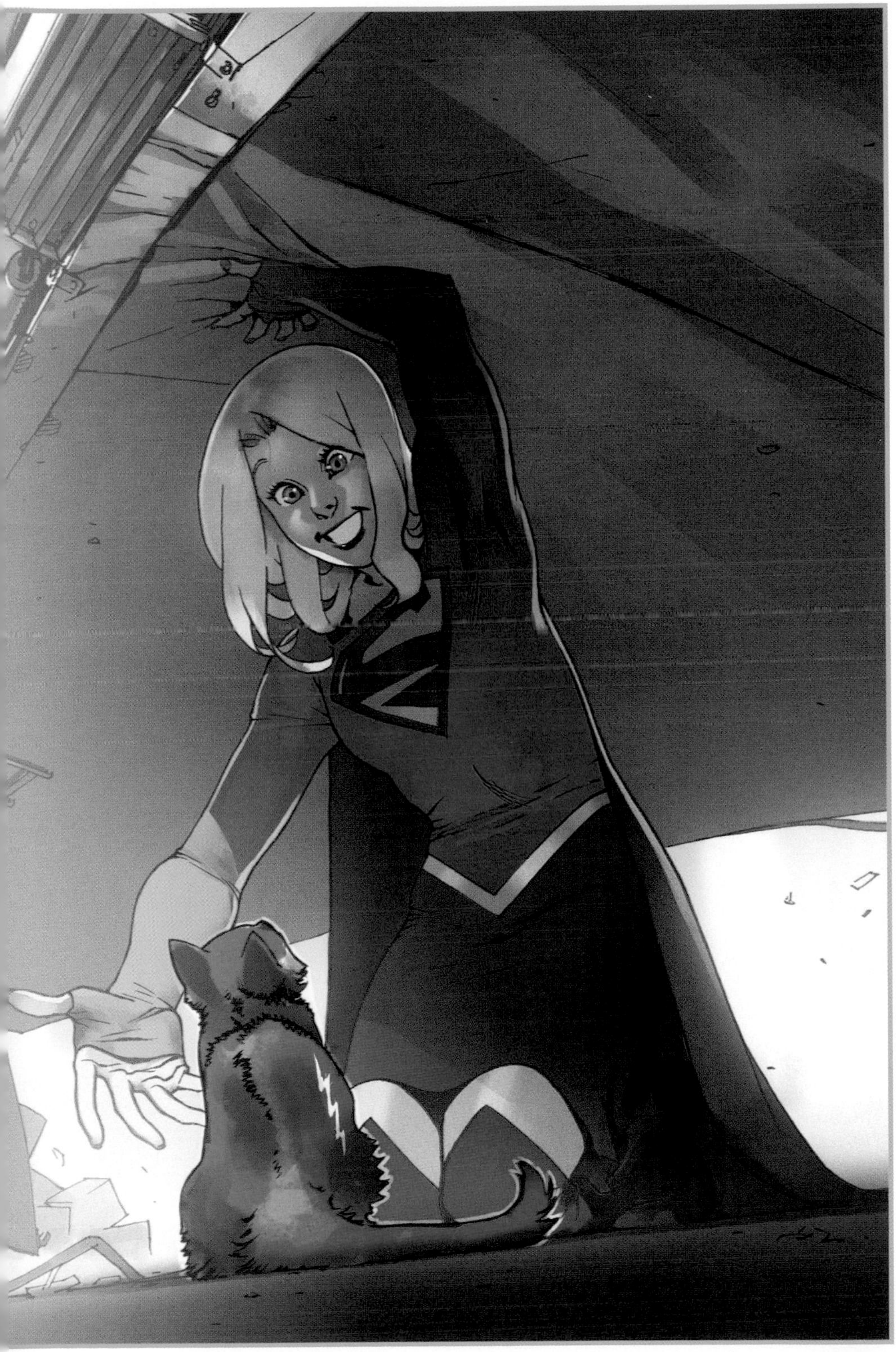

Krypto the
Super-Dog

# Super-Pets

Krypto is Superman and Supergirl's dog. He
is no ordinary dog; he is also a Super-Pet!
Krypto was named after Supergirl's home
planet, Krypton. He uses super–smell power
to sniff out villains from miles away.
Sometimes Krypto comes to the rescue
when Supergirl is in a tight spot. Krypto is
the most loyal dog in the whole galaxy.

Supergirl's pet horse is named Comet. Comet was given his powers by a witch, who cast a spell on him. Now Comet can fly as high as Supergirl.

**Comet the Super-Horse**

# Batgirl

Barbara Gordon is a young woman from Gotham City. There is lots of crime there. Barbara's father, Commissioner Gordon, is the head of the police. Barbara wanted to help protect her city. She became the Super Hero Batgirl. Now Batgirl's crime fighting inspires others to do good.

Batgirl and Supergirl defeated an evil villain named Magog together. Batgirl helps Supergirl to believe in herself. That's what friends are for!

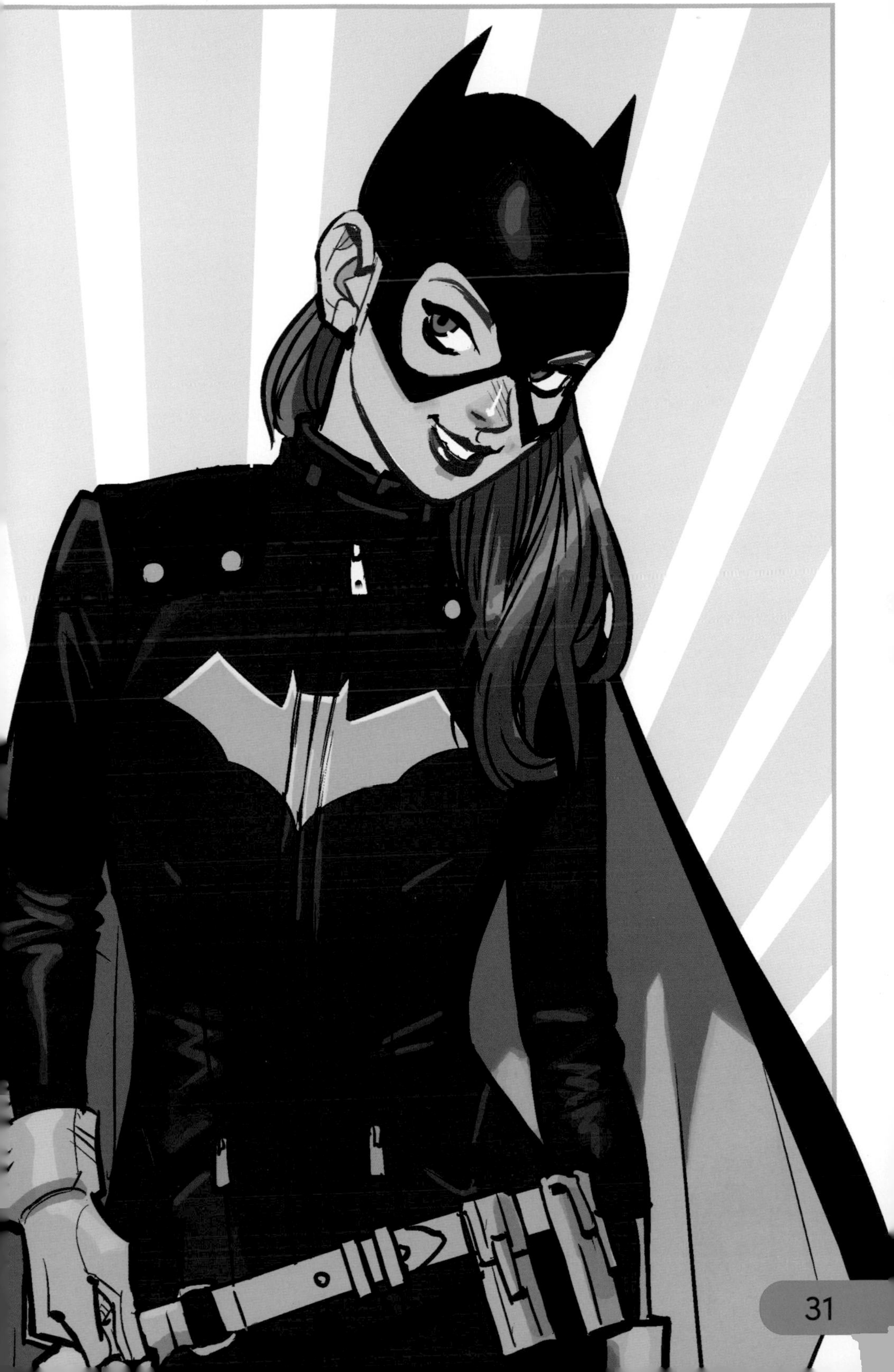

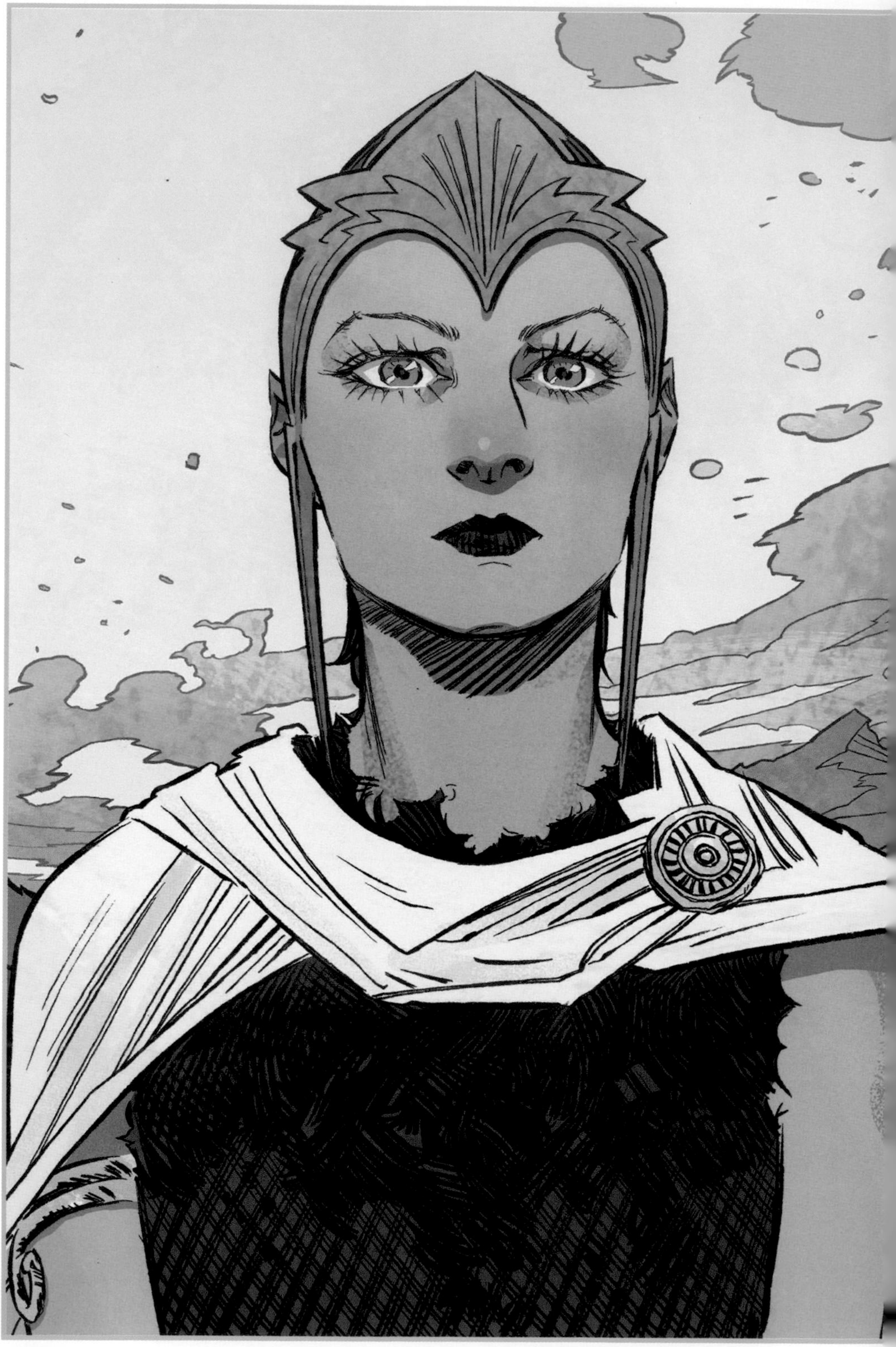

# Ruthye

Ruthye is a young girl who comes from a planet with a red sun. Ruthye has purple eyes. She is Supergirl's ally and friend. Together they have traveled across the galaxy. Ruthye is honest and loyal.

# Power Girl

In another universe, Supergirl is known as Power Girl. Power Girl lives on a planet named Earth-2. Power Girl has the same superpowers as Supergirl. However, she is older, with more knowledge of the universe.

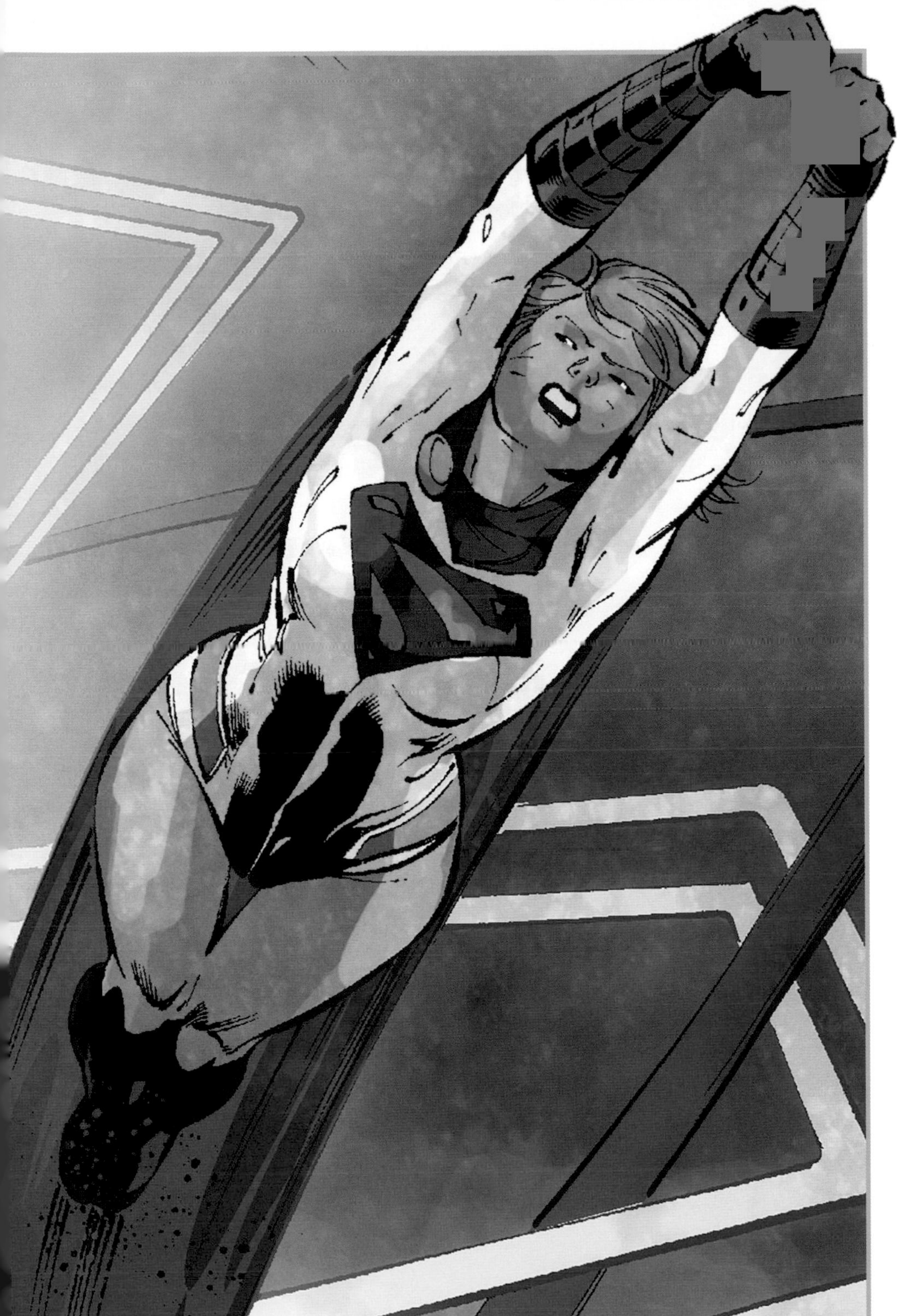

# Superman's family

Lois Lane is a journalist at the *Daily Planet* newspaper. She is very caring and clever. She is married to Superman. Together they have a son, Jon Kent. Jon has superpowers, too. He makes his parents very proud.

Kara loves spending time with Superman and his family. Everyone needs someone to look out for them; even Super Heroes.

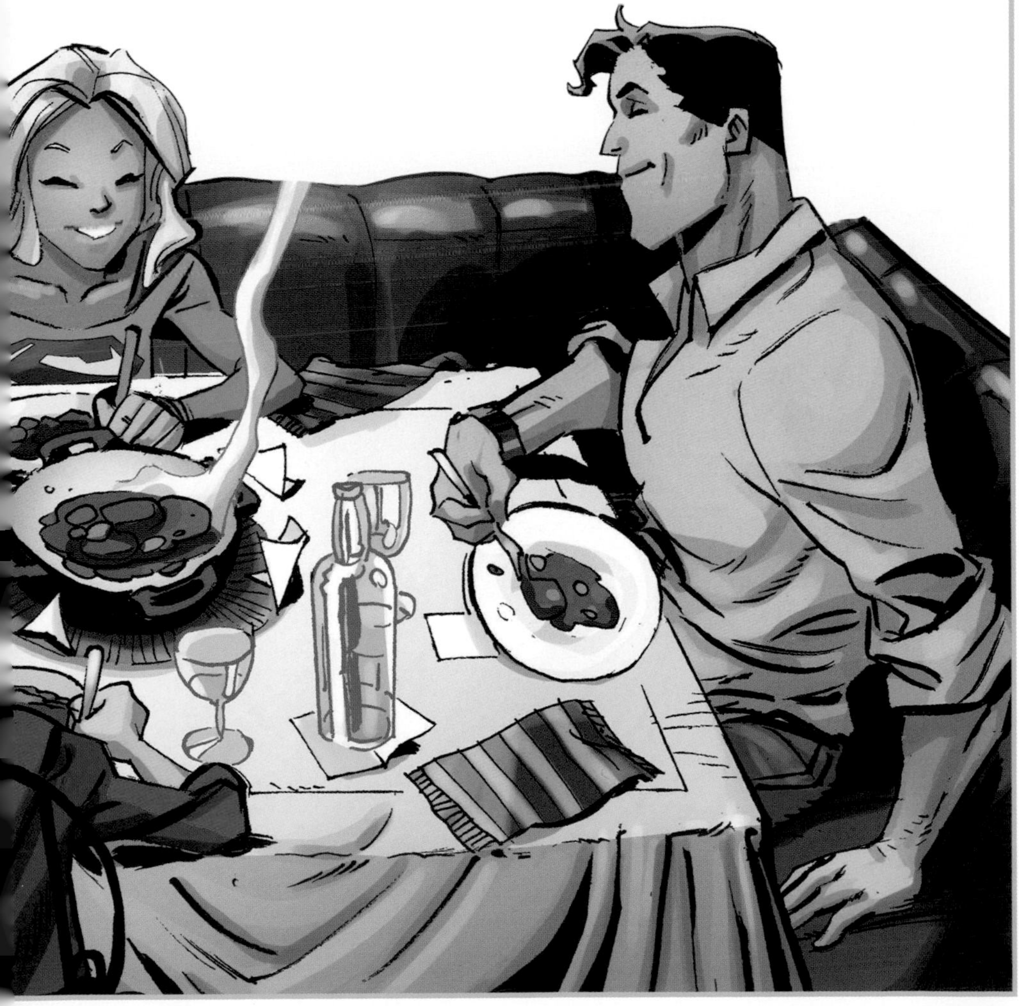

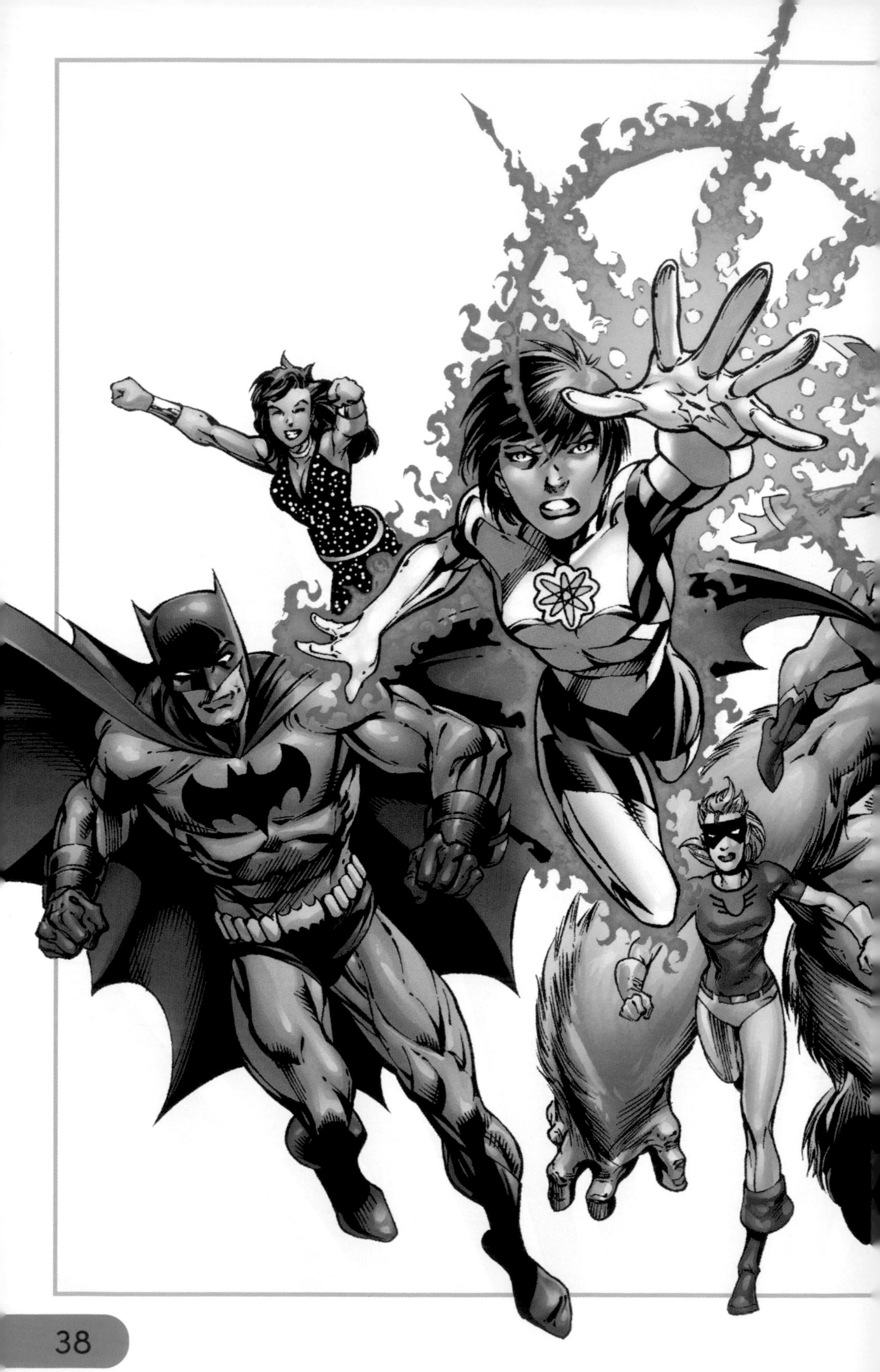

# Justice League

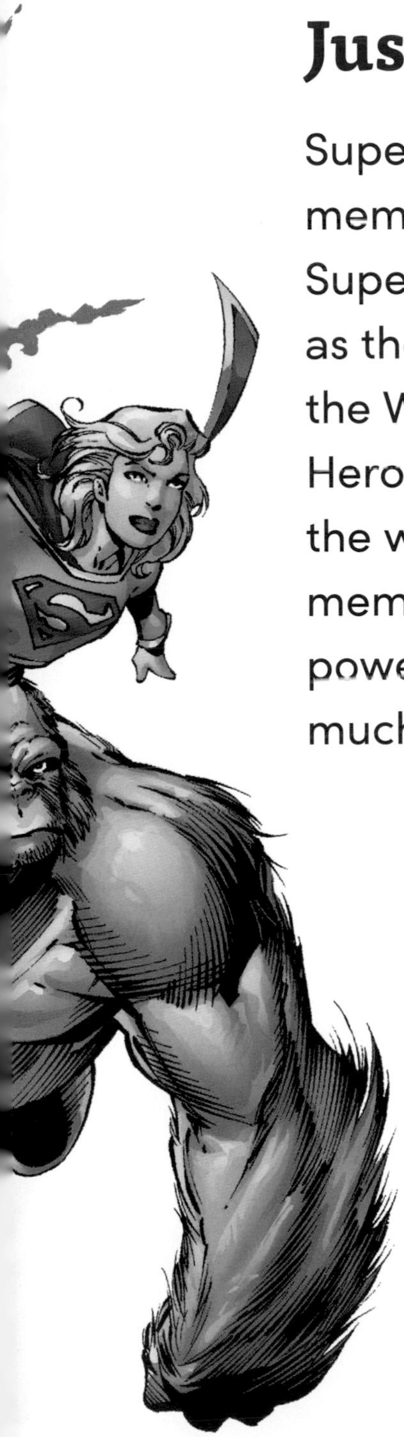

Supergirl is an important member of a famous group of Super Heroes. They are known as the Justice League, and are the World's Greatest Super Heroes. Together they protect the world from evil. Each member of the Justice League is powerful alone, but they are much stronger as a team.

# Cyborg Superman

Supergirl often has to fight to protect her friends. When Kara's home city, Argo, on Krypton was destroyed, Kara's father used evil technology to save himself and his people. He became Cyborg Superman. He wanted to save Argo by destroying National City. Kara could not let this happen. To save her new home, Supergirl had to defeat Cyborg Superman.

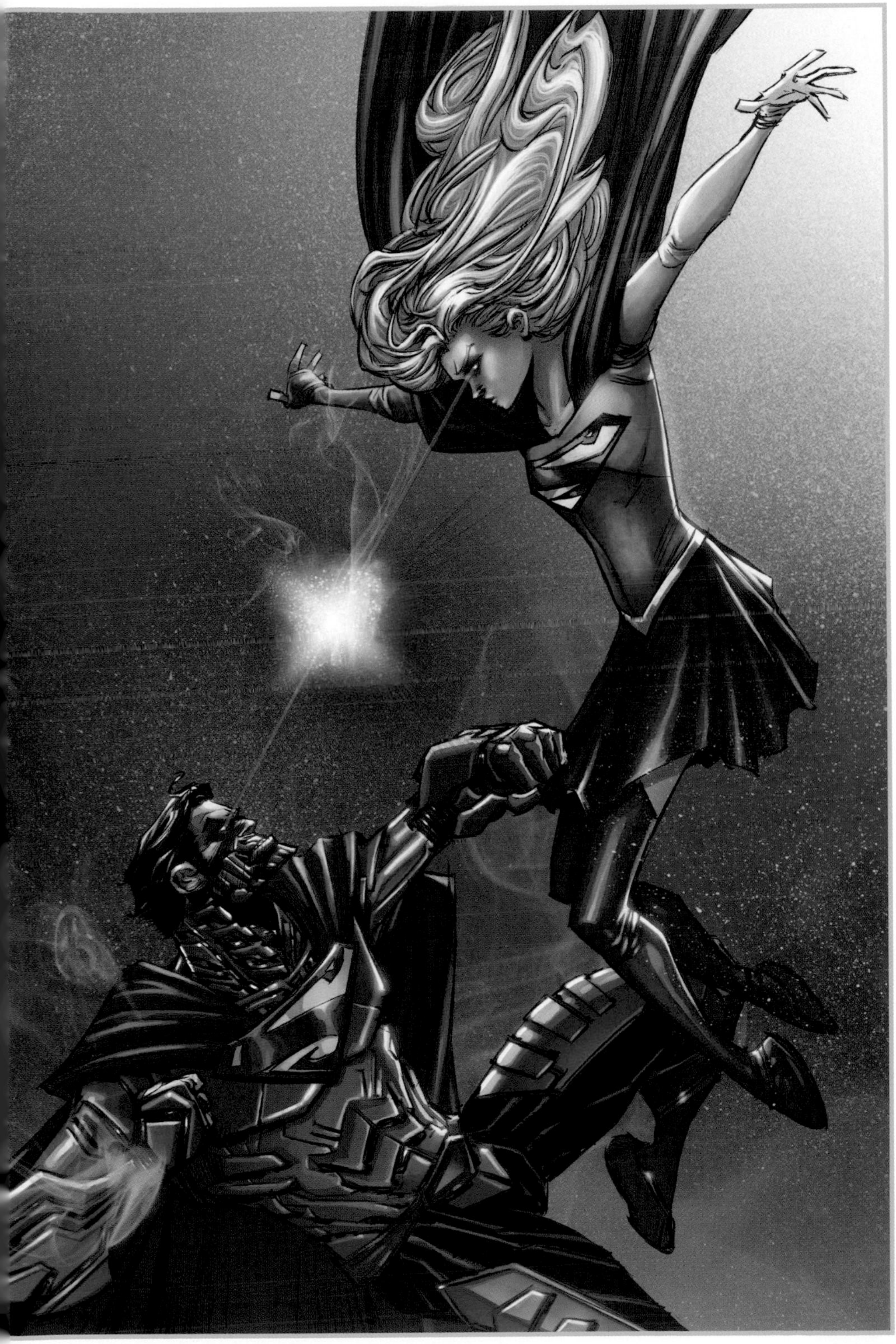

# Rogol Zaar

Rogol Zaar is an evil alien monster. He wanted to destroy all Kryptonians. He hunted for Supergirl and Superman and fought with Superman in space. Supergirl came to Superman's rescue. She trapped Rogol Zaar in a prison where he couldn't hurt anyone. Supergirl tries to stop her enemies without using violence.

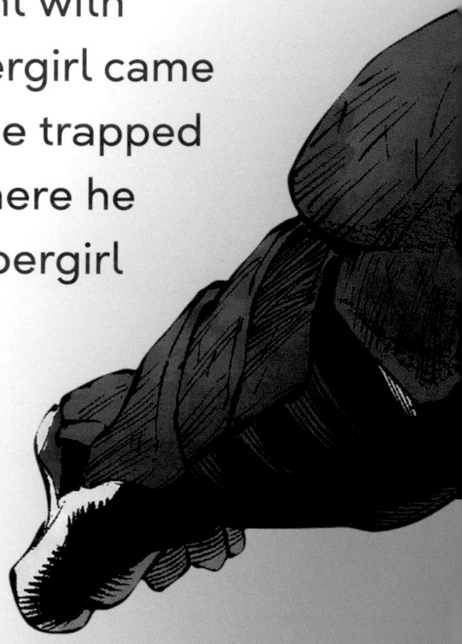

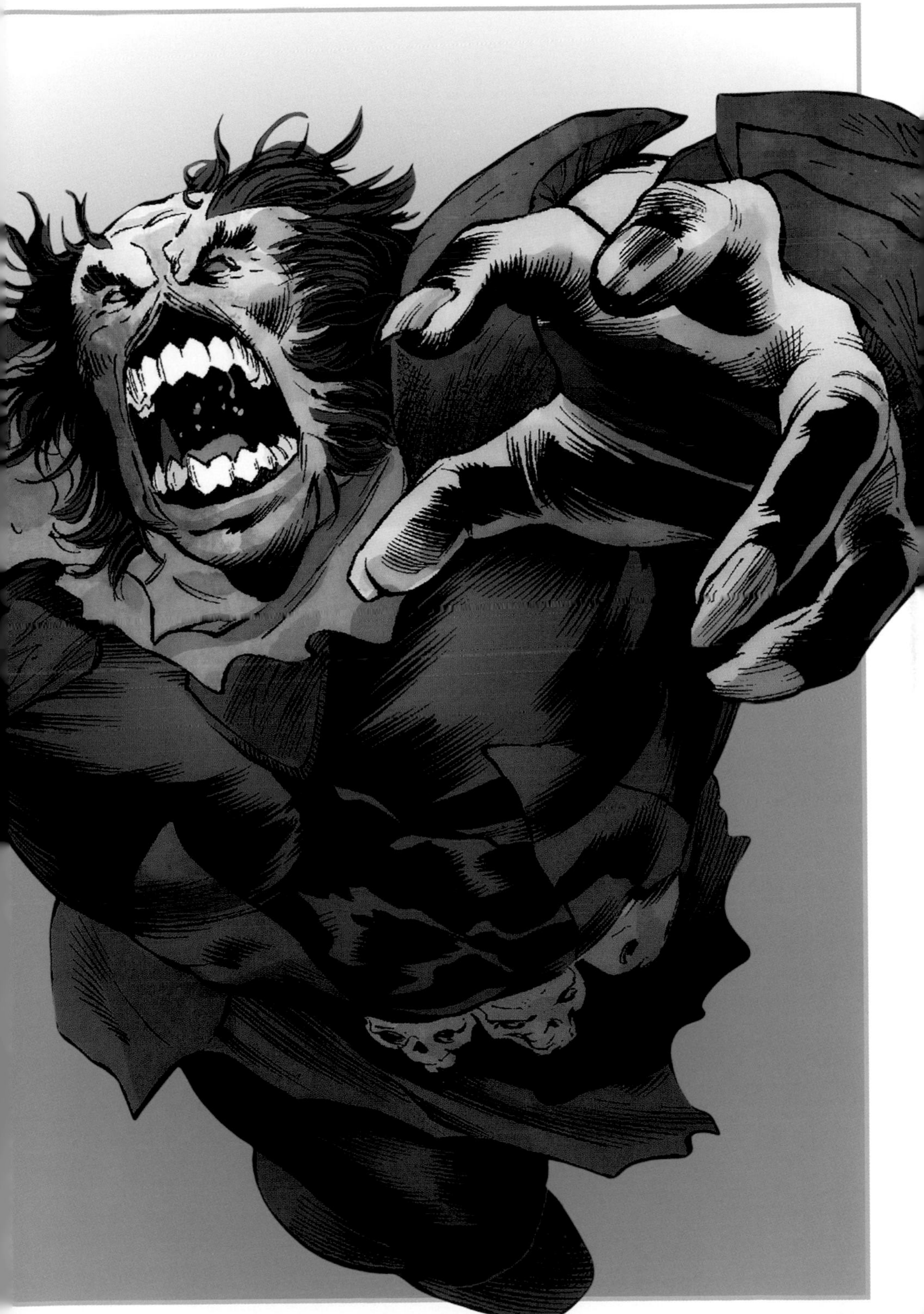

# Saving the city

Supergirl's motto is "hope, compassion and help for all."

When people are in danger, Supergirl is there to help. Despite her powers, what really makes Supergirl a Super Hero is her bravery.

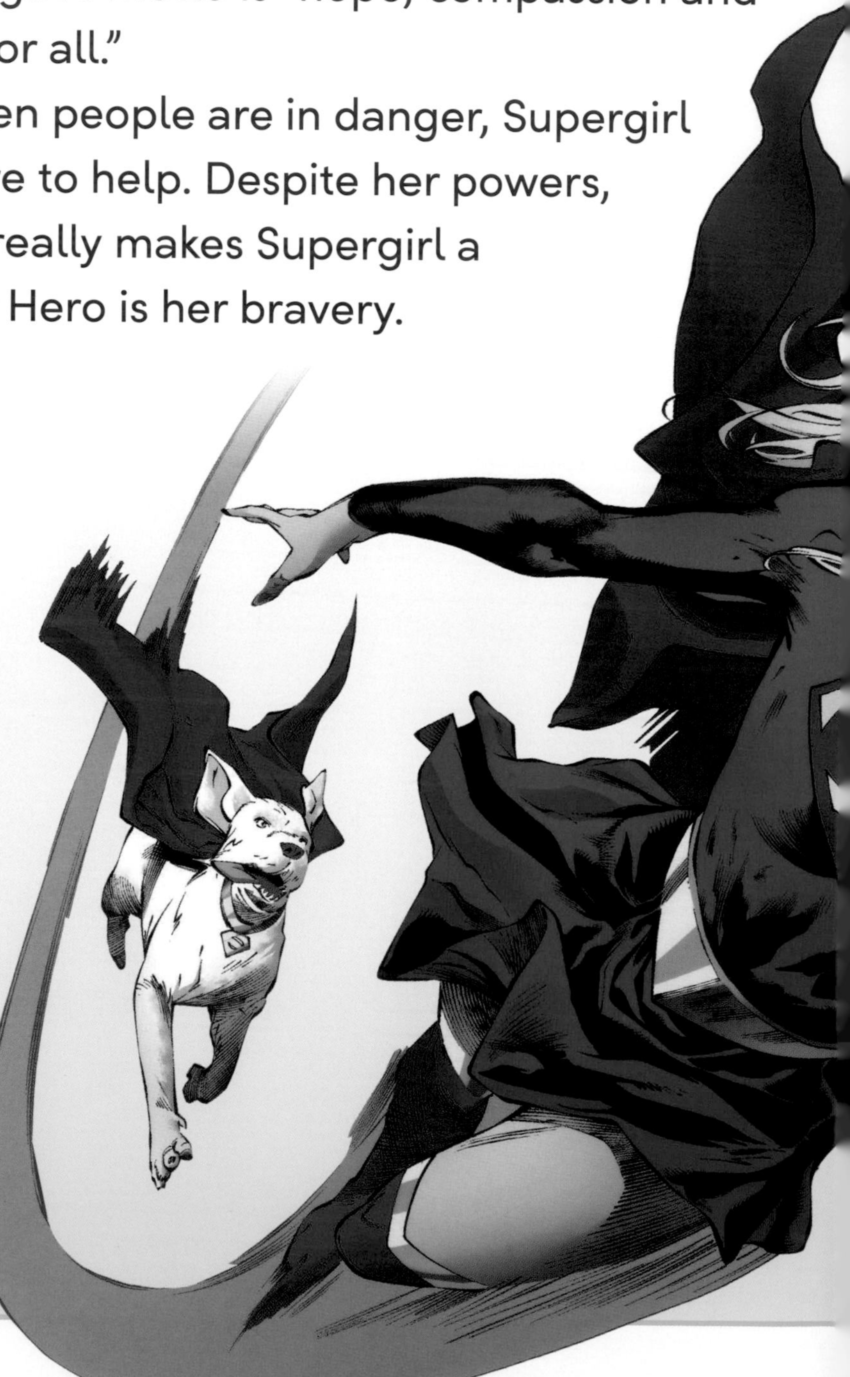

National City and the Universe, can count on Supergirl. She will always try to save the day!

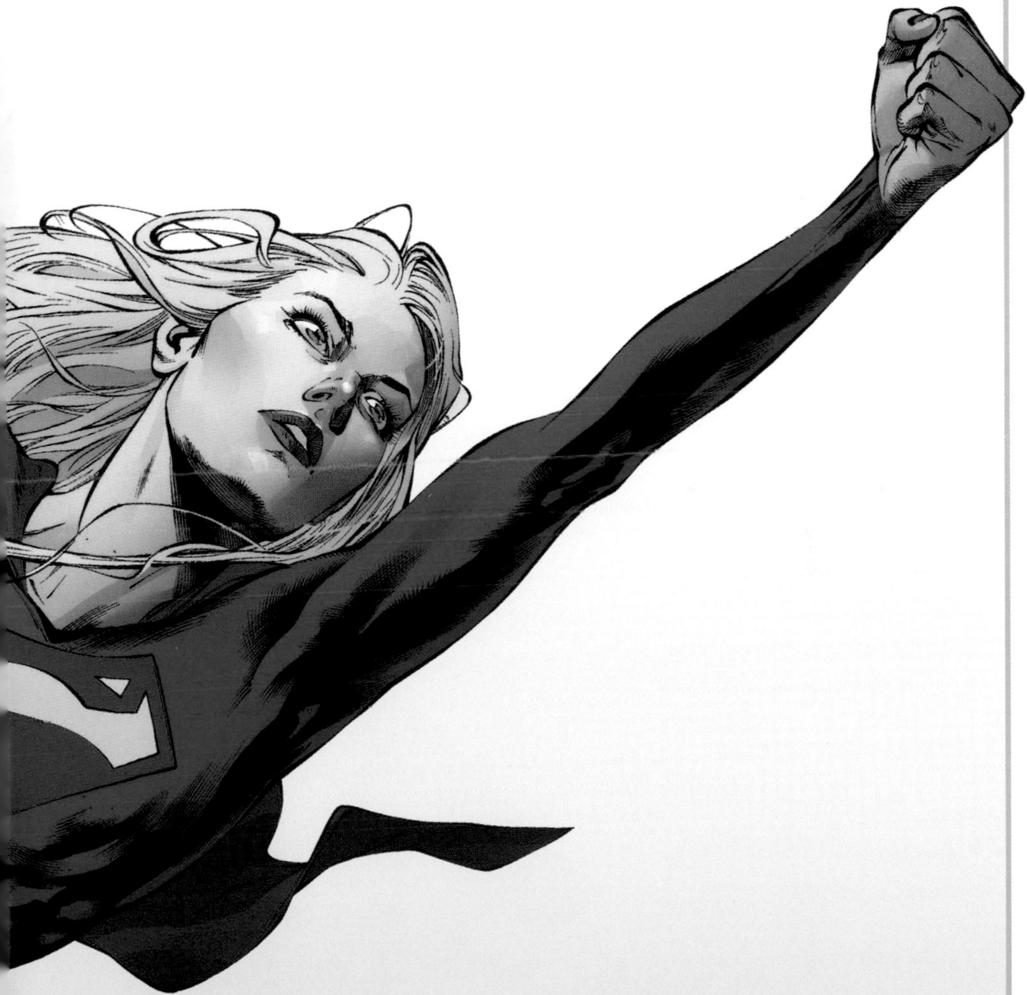

# Glossary

**ally**
someone who gives help and support to an important cause

**Commissioner**
a person who is in charge of a police force

**cyborg**
someone that is part human and part machine

**department**
one part of a large organization

**explosion**
a sudden burst of energy that can cause lots of damage

**foster parents**
people who take a child into their family for a period of time

**gifted**
having amazing talents or abilities

**identity**
who a person is

**journalist**
a person who reports the news and current events

**missions**
tasks that someone must perform

**steel**
a strong metal

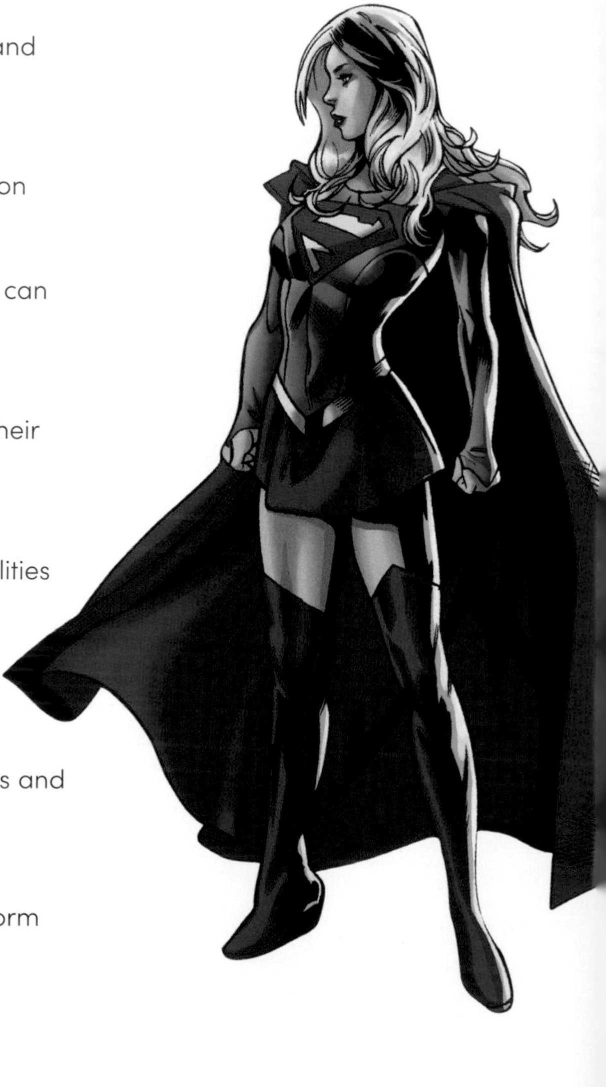

# Index

# Quiz

What have you learned about Supergirl and her friends?

1.   What is the name of Supergirl's home planet?

2.   In which city does Supergirl live on Earth?

3.   What mark does Streaky the Super-Cat have on his fur?

4.   What color are Ruthye's eyes?

5.   Which newspaper does Lois Lane work for?

1. Krypton  2. National City  3. A lightning bolt  4. Purple  5. The *Daily Planet*